Possum Magic

WRITTEN BY
Mem Fox

ILLUSTRATED BY
Julie Vivas

HARCOURT, INC.
Orlando   Austin   New York   San Diego   London

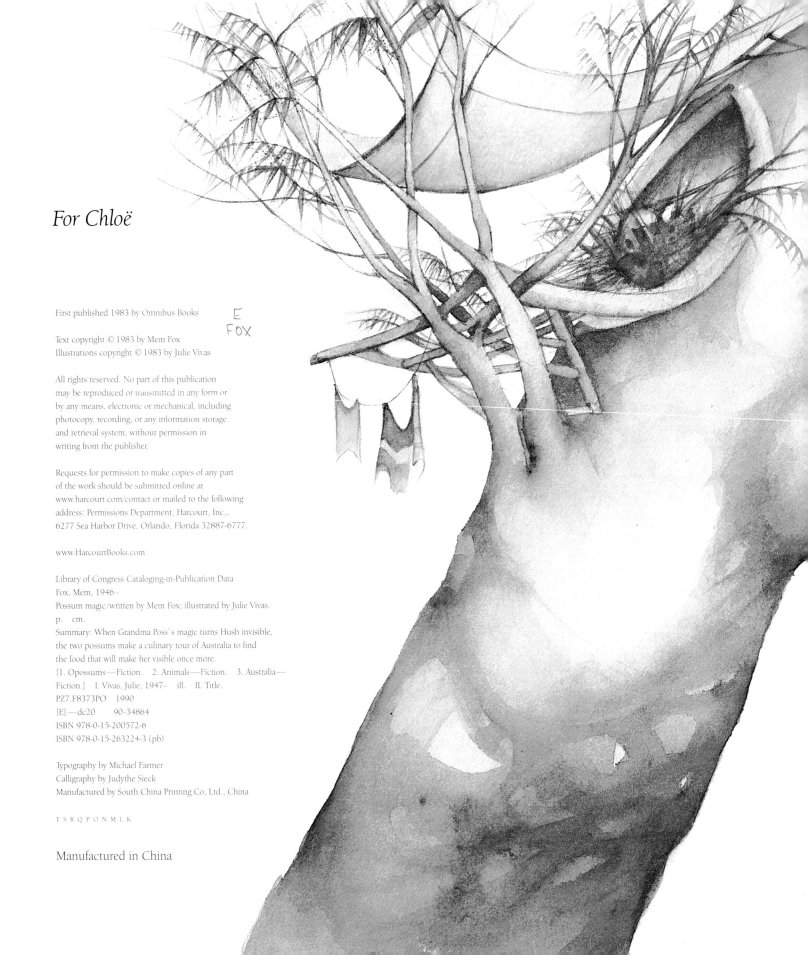

For Chloë

First published 1983 by Omnibus Books

E
FOX

Text copyright © 1983 by Mem Fox
Illustrations copyright © 1983 by Julie Vivas

Requests for permission to make copies of any part
of the work should be submitted online at
www.harcourt.com/contact or mailed to the following
address: Permissions Department, Harcourt, Inc.,
6277 Sea Harbor Drive, Orlando, Florida 32887-6777.

www.HarcourtBooks.com

Library of Congress Cataloging-in-Publication Data
Fox, Mem, 1946–
Possum magic/written by Mem Fox; illustrated by Julie Vivas.
p.   cm.
Summary: When Grandma Poss's magic turns Hush invisible,
the two possums make a culinary tour of Australia to find
the food that will make her visible once more.
[1. Opossums—Fiction.   2. Animals—Fiction.   3. Australia—
Fiction.]   I. Vivas, Julie, 1947–   ill.   II. Title.
PZ7.F8373PO   1990
[E]—dc20   90-34864
ISBN 978-0-15-200572-6
ISBN 978-0-15-263224-3 (pb)

Typography by Michael Farmer
Calligraphy by Judythe Sieck
Manufactured by South China Printing Co, Ltd., China

T S R Q P O N M L K

Manufactured in China

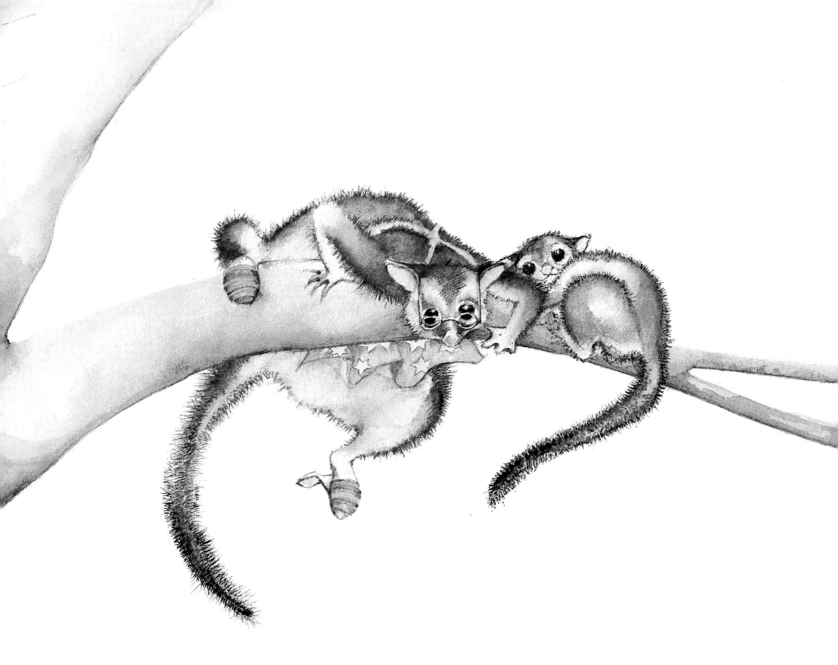

Once upon a time, but not very long ago,
deep in the Australian bush lived two possums.
Their names were Hush and Grandma Poss.

Grandma Poss made bush magic.
She made wombats blue
and kookaburras pink.
She made dingoes smile
and emus shrink.
But the best magic of all . . .

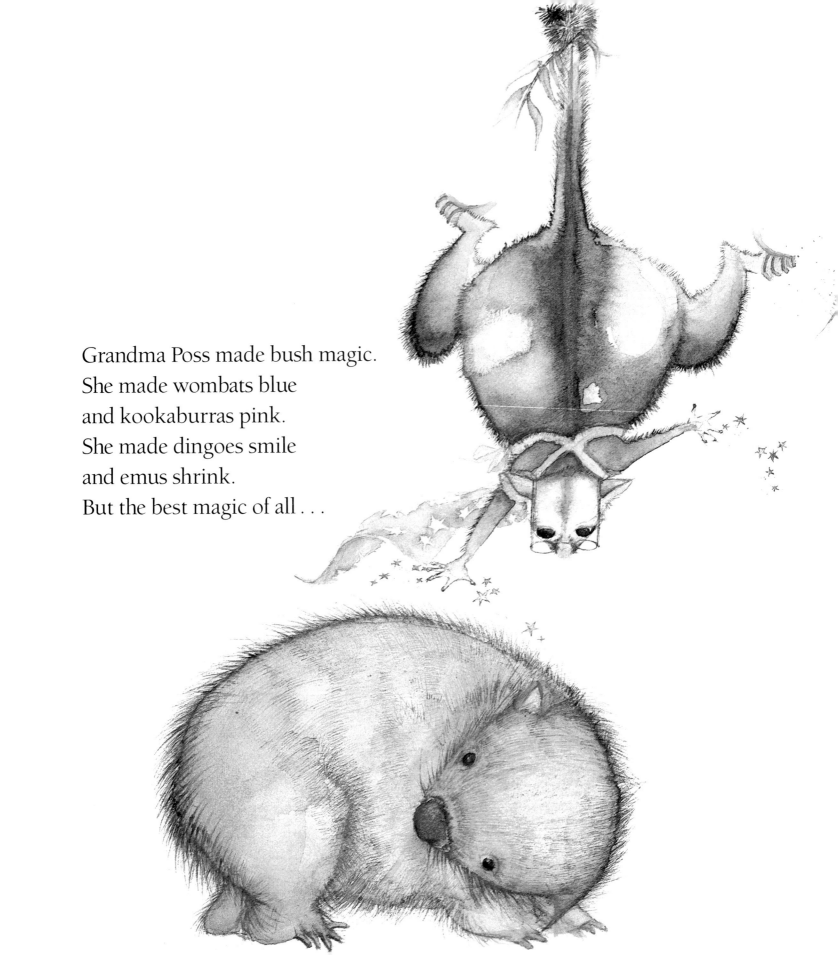

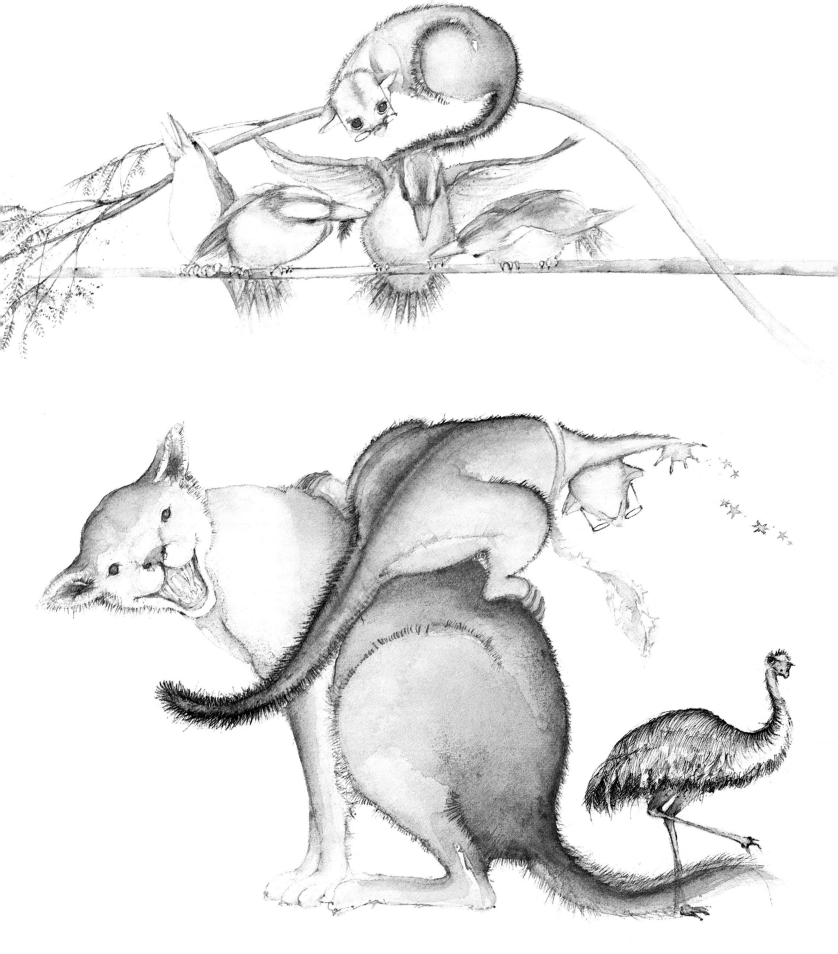

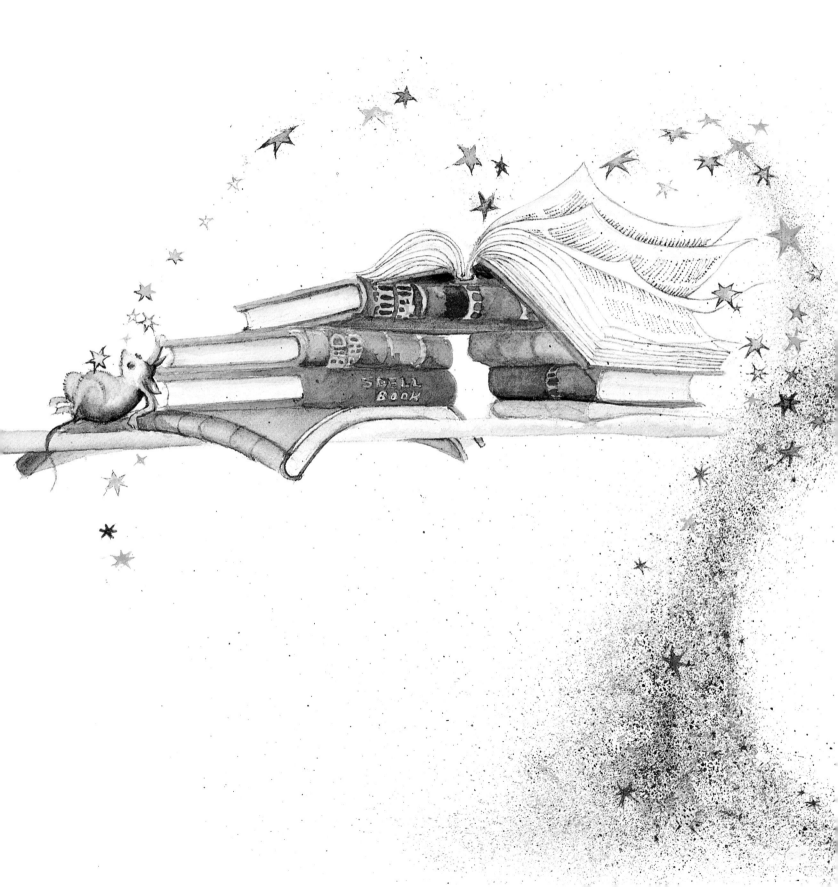

was the magic that made Hush *invisible*.

What adventures Hush had!
Because she couldn't be seen,
she could be squashed by koalas.

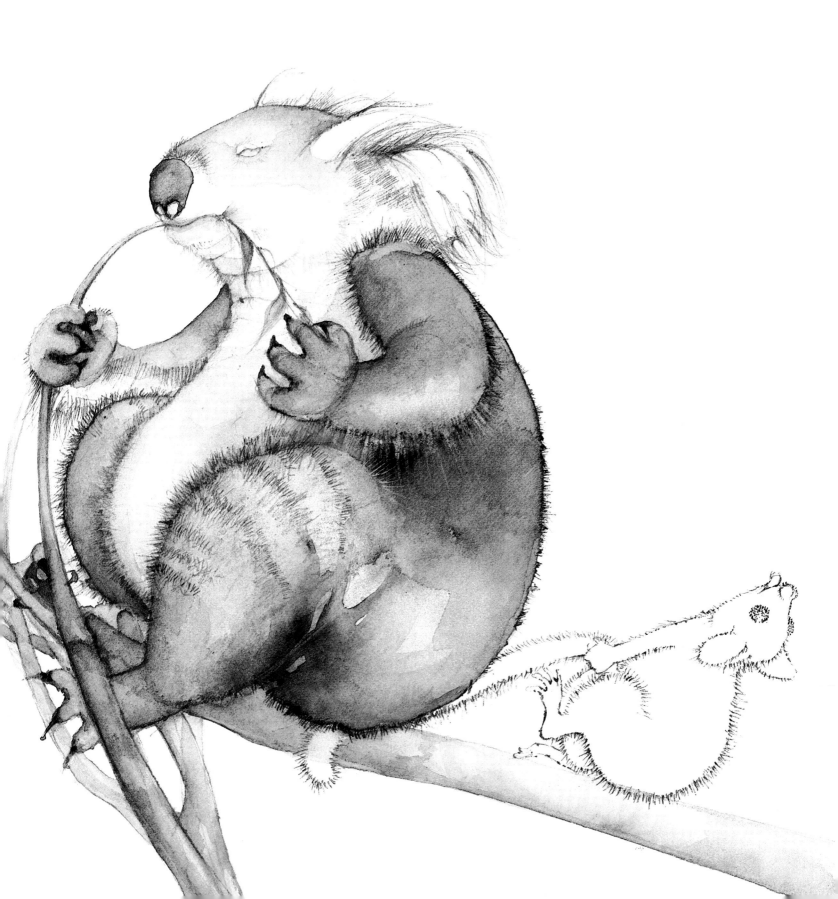

Because she couldn't be seen, she could slide down kangaroos.

Because she couldn't be seen, she was safe from snakes,
which is why Grandma Poss had made her invisible in the first place.

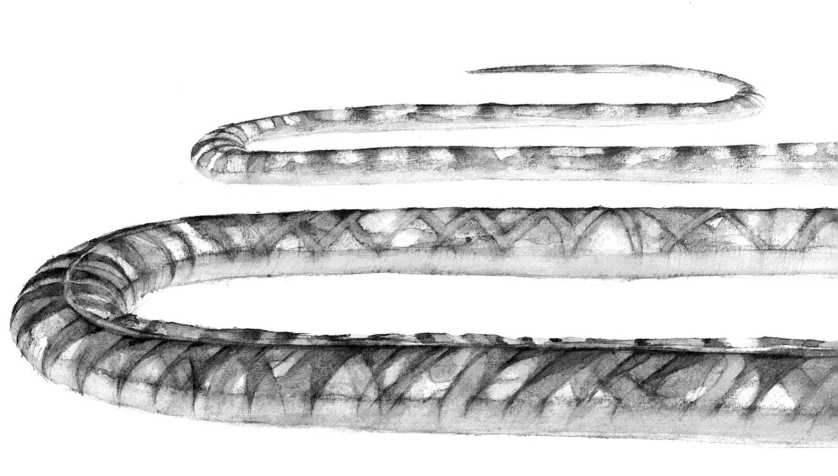

But one day, quite unexpectedly, Hush said,
"Grandma, I want to know what I look like.
Please could you make me visible again?"
"Of course I can," said Grandma Poss,
and she began to look through her magic books.

She looked into this book and she looked into that.
There was magic for thin and magic for fat,
magic for tall and magic for small,
but the magic she was looking for wasn't there at all.

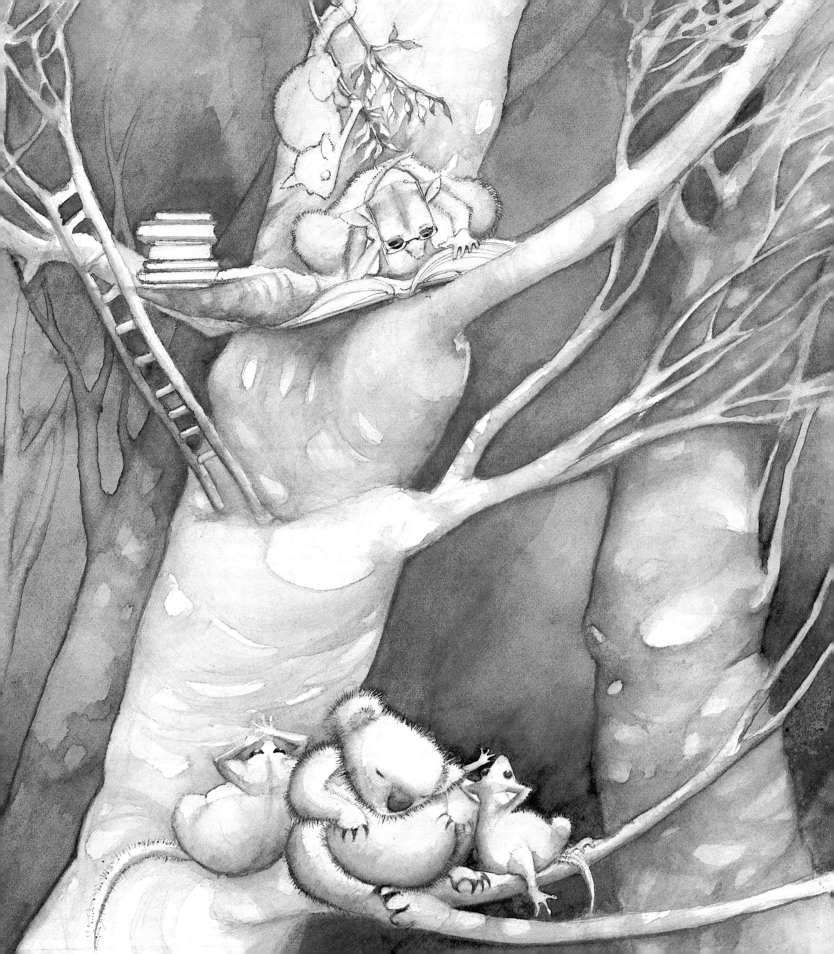

Grandma Poss looked miserable.
"Don't worry, Grandma," said Hush.
"I don't mind."

But in her heart of hearts she did.

All night long Grandma Poss thought and thought.
The next morning, just before breakfast, she shouted,
"It's something to do with food! People food — not
possum food. But I can't remember what.
We'll just have to try and find it."

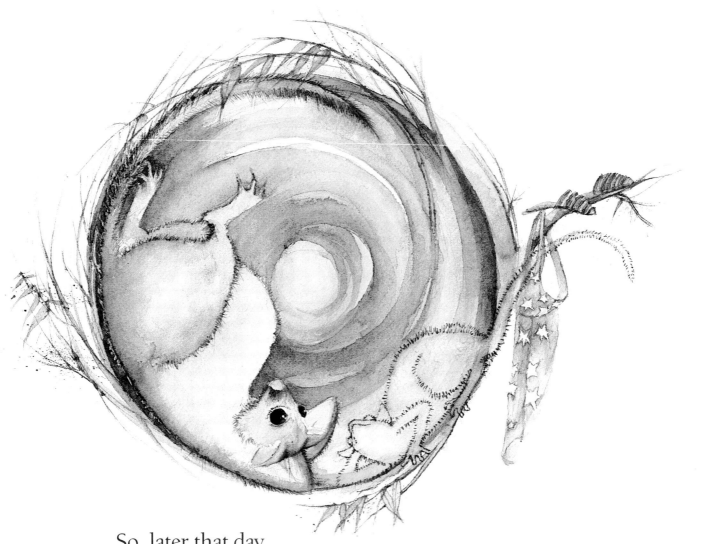

So, later that day,
they left the bush where they'd always been
to find what it was that would make Hush seen.

They ate Anzac biscuits in Adelaide,
mornay and Minties in Melbourne,
steak and salad in Sydney,
and pumpkin scones in Brisbane.

Hush remained invisible.
"Don't lose heart!" said Grandma Poss.
"Let's see what we can find in Darwin."

It was there, in the far north of Australia,
that they found a Vegemite sandwich.
Grandma Poss crossed her claws and crossed her feet.
Hush breathed deeply and began to eat.
"A tail! A tail!" shouted both possums at once.
For there it was. A brand-new, visible tail.

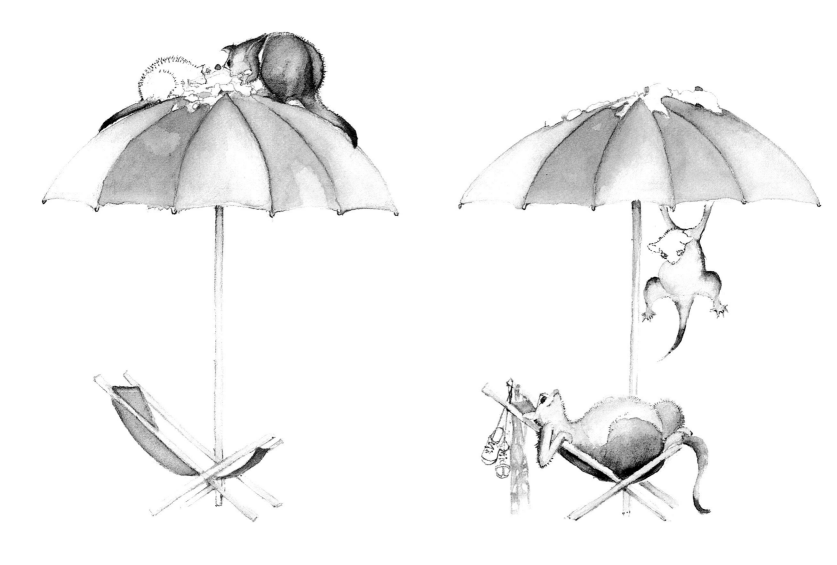

Later, on a beach in Perth, they ate a piece of pavlova.
Hush's legs appeared. So did her body.
"You look wonderful, you precious possum!" said Grandma Poss.
"Next stop — Tasmania."
And over the sea they went.

In Hobart, late one night, in the kitchens
of the casino, they saw a lamington on a plate.
Hush closed her eyes and nibbled.
Grandma Poss held her breath and waited.

"It's worked! It's worked!" she cried.
And she was right.
Hush could be seen from head to tail.
Grandma Poss hugged Hush, and they both
danced "Here We Go Round the Lamington Plate"
till early in the morning.

From that time onward Hush was visible.
But once a year, on her birthday, she and Grandma Poss
ate a Vegemite sandwich, a piece of pavlova, and half
a lamington, just to make sure that Hush stayed visible forever.

And she did.

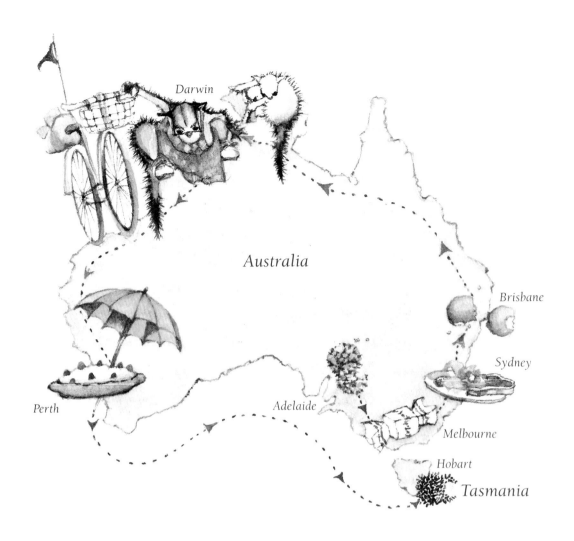

Darwin

Australia

Brisbane

Sydney

Perth

Adelaide

Melbourne

Hobart

Tasmania

GLOSSARY OF AUSTRALIAN TERMS

ANZAC BISCUITS:
traditional rolled-oat and syrup cookies

MORNAY:
a supper dish of fish in white sauce, topped with bread crumbs and browned in the oven

MINTIES:
peppermint-flavored nougat candies

VEGEMITE:
a salty yeast spread used on toast and in sandwiches

PAVLOVA:
a meringue shell topped with fresh fruits and whipped cream

LAMINGTON:
a square of sponge cake dipped in thin chocolate icing and rolled in coconut